Cat was curled up nearby.

"Climb over the wall," she purred.

"It's beautiful on the other side. I could

jump over in a jiffy, but you're s-o-o-o slow!"

And she jumped over the wall.

Snail slid slowly on

He was one brick up the wall when Wasp flew by.

"What's the matter, Snail?" buzzed Wasp.

"I'm hot," said Snail, "and hungry."

"Keep going," said Wasp. "It's beautiful

on the other side. I could buzz over in a trice,

but you're s-o-o-o slow!" And he buzzed over

the wall.

Snail slid slowly on.

Snail was two bricks up the wall when Butterfly

fluttered past.

"What's the matter, Snail?" warbled Butterfly.

"I'm hot and hungry," said Snail. "I'm thirsty, too."

"Keep going," said Butterfly. "It's beautiful on

the other side. Of course, I could flit over in a flash,

but you're s-o-o-o slow!" And she fluttered over

the wall.

Snail slid slowly on.

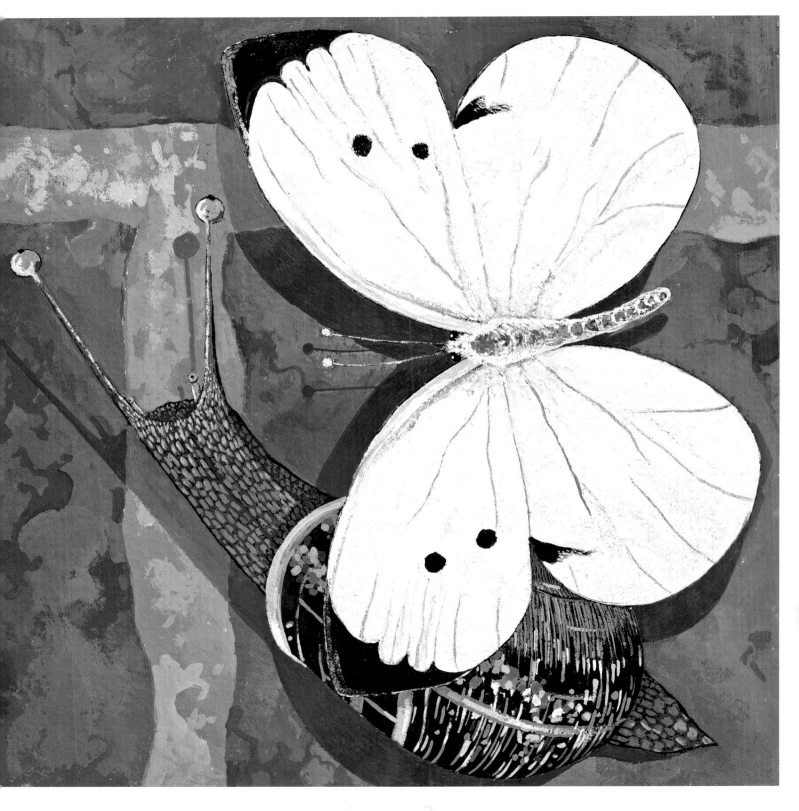

Snail was three bricks up the wall when suddenly

he found himself in a terrible tangle.

"You've broken my new web!" spluttered Spider.

"So sorry," said Snail, "but I must find some shade."

"Keep going," said Spider. "It's beautiful on the

other side. Of course, I could scuttle over in a second,

but you're s-o-o-o slow!" And he scuttled over

the wall.

Snail slid slowly on.

Snail was sitting very still, when Centipede

scurried by.

"What's the matter, Snail?" called Centipede.

"I can't go any further," whispered Snail.

"Of course you can!" said Centipede. "I know

a secret." And he showed snail a small, dark hole

between two bricks.

"Come on," said Centipede. "Follow me."

At last they came to the other side.

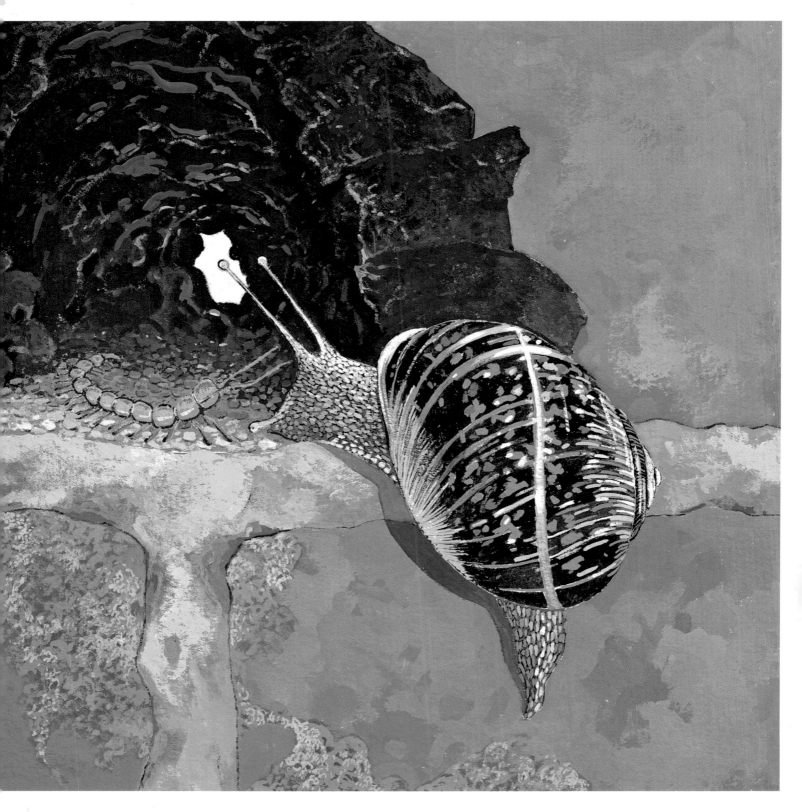

There, below them, was a wonderful surprise:

a cool, shady orchard with beautiful green grass.

"Oh!" cried Snail in delight.

"You'll be all right now," said Centipede,

scurrying off.

But as Snail began sliding down

towards the soft green grass,

a dark shadow fell across him.

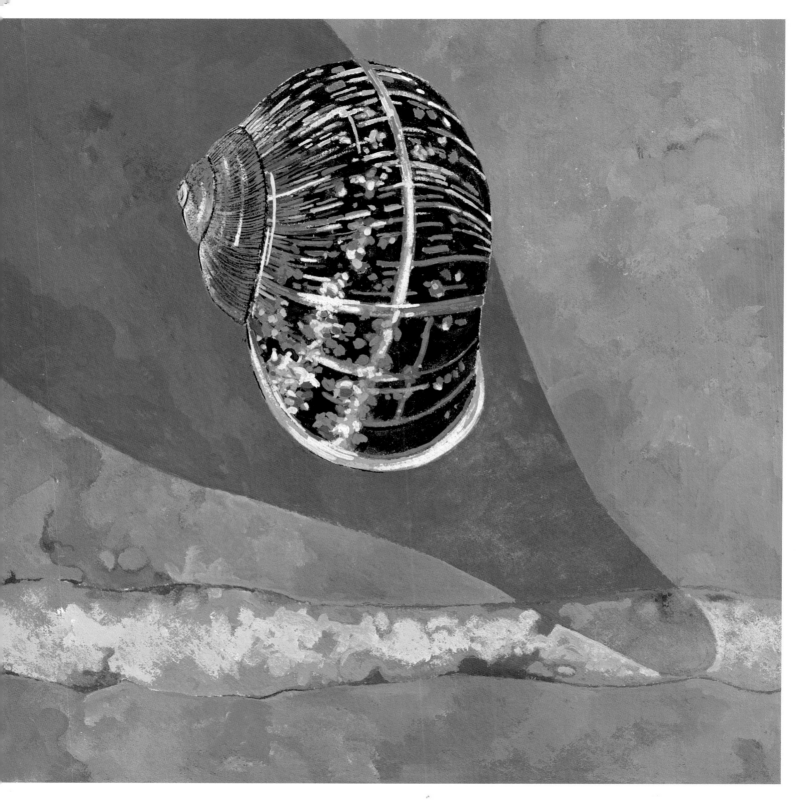

It was Bird.

Snail shrank into his shell

as the shape grew larger and larger.

Bird was just about to swoop when...

Up pounced Cat!

Bird squawked and flew away.

Snail was safe at last.

In the orchard, Spider, Butterfly, Wasp and Cat were talking.

"Poor old Snail," laughed Cat. "He's s-o-o-o slow.

He'll never get here."

But then they saw some leaves moving. . .

"Oh, Snail," they cried. "You're not so slow after all!"

There was Snail, contentedly munching a delicious green leaf. He looked up and smiled.

"Slow but sure!" he said.

So Slow! © Frances Lincoln Ltd 2001
Text and Illustrations copyright © Dave and Julie Saunders 2001

First published in Great Britain in 2001 by Frances Lincoln Limited,
4 Torriano Mews, Torriano Avenue, London, NW5 2RZ

British Library Cataloguing in Publication Data available on request

ISBN 0-7112-1667-3

Printed in Hong Kong

1 3 5 7 9 8 6 4 2